Home Base

Jeff Gerke

D1603469

Angela Hunt, Alton Gansky,
and Bill Myers

JEFF GERKE

Published by Amaris Media International.
Copyright © 2016 Jeff Gerke
Cover Design: Angela Hunt
Photo credits: © nexusseven – fotolia.com

ISBN-13: 978-0692731499
ISBN-10: 0692731490

For more information, visit us on Facebook:
https://www.facebook.com/pages/Harbingers/705107309586877

or *www.harbingersseries.com*.

HARBINGERS

A novella series by
Bill Myers, Jeff Gerke, Angela Hunt,
and Alton Gansky

In this fast-paced world with all its demands, the four of us wanted to try something new. Instead of the longer novel format, we wanted to write something equally as engaging but that could be read in one or two sittings—on the plane, waiting to pick up the kids from soccer, or as an evening's read.

We also wanted to play. As friends and seasoned novelists, we thought it would be fun to create a game we could participate in together. The rules were simple:

Rule #1

Each of us will write as if we were one of the characters in the series:

Bill Myers will write as Brenda, the street-hustling tattoo artist who sees images of the future.

Frank Peretti will write as the professor, the atheist ex-priest ruled by logic.

Jeff Gerke will write as Chad, the mind reader with devastating good looks and an arrogance to match.

Angela Hunt will write as Andi, the brilliant-but-geeky young woman who sees inexplicable patterns.

Alton Gansky will write as Tank, the naïve, big-hearted jock with a surprising connection to a healing power.

Rule #2

Instead of the five of us writing one novella

together (we're friends but not crazy), we would write it like a TV series. There would be an overarching storyline into which we'd plug our individual novellas, with each story written from our character's point of view.

If you're keeping track, this is the order:

Harbingers #1—*The Call*—Bill Myers
Harbingers #2—*The Haunt*ed—Frank Peretti
Harbingers #3—*The Sentinels*—Angela Hunt
Harbingers #4—*The Girl*—Alton Gansky

Volumes #1-4 omnibus: *Cycle One: Invitation*

Harbingers #5—*The Revealing*—Bill Myers
Harbingers #6—*Infestation*—Frank Peretti
Harbingers #7—*Infiltration*—Angela Hunt
Harbingers #8—*The Fog*—Alton Gansky

Volumes #5-8 omnibus: *Cycle Two: Mosaic*

Harbingers #9—*Leviathan*—Bill Myers
Harbingers #10—*The Mind Pirates*—Frank Peretti
Harbingers #11—*Hybrids*—Angela Hunt
Harbingers #12—*The Village*—Alton Gansky

Volumes 9-12 omnibus: *Cycle Three: The Probing*

Harbingers #13—*Piercing the Veil*—Bill Myers
Harbingers #14—*Home Base*—Jeff Gerke

There you have it, at least for now. We hope you'll find these as entertaining in the reading as we are in the writing.

Bill, Jeff, Angie, and Al

SMARTMOUTH AND THE KID

I suppose I should try to rescue her. She *did* save my life, after all. Technically.

Whatever. Okay, fine.

I used the remote control to dim the windows and shut the drapes. Couldn't see much over the Dallas haze today anyway, even from the top floor. But I could still hear the jets taking off, and I probably needed to concentrate. Imminent death to the smartmouth, the kid, and the troll, and all that. And to beautiful Andi.

Yeah, okay. But first things first.

I crossed the living room of my suite—all white fabric and chrome appointments—and went into my white chromy bedroom. I propped the pillows around the headboard and sat up on the bed against them. I shut my eyes and went through the descent protocol.

Right away, I saw the black horizon with a billion options to choose from. It always reminded me of sitting in the middle of a huge black lake and seeing the lights of houses and villages here and there all around me. I thought about the photos of the kid— Daniel or whatever—and saw one of the dots flare at the edge of the blackness. I imagined myself closer to it, and there he was.

Nobody around to say I'd told 'em so, but a pack of black-eyed peas had already surrounded Daniel and were about to strike. In my remote viewing vision, they looked like loose clumps of cloth circling in well water. But I knew they were guided by an intelligent evil in their attack on the kid.

Which meant Brenda, a.k.a., Smartmouth, was probably in danger, too.

Yeah, there she was, flaring nearby in the fog. I might be able to get her attention even now, without training, but Daniel was more open. Plus … imminent death and all.

Hey, kid, I thought at him. *It's me, Chad Thorton. You hear me?*

I got a flash of Daniel—skinny geek kid. Pale skin. Typical brainiac. How well I knew what the future held for him. The gestalt I received showed him playing a video game in front of a TV.

Hi, Chad.

I had to smile. The kid was good. Quick answer. No apparent strain. Definitely gifted, this one. *You know me?*

An impression of a shrug, plus the TV turning off.

Brenda told me. What's up?

My vision was clearing and everything looked almost like reality. I could see their cluttered and tiny home. Every now and then my sight fritzed out and I saw nothing or a glimpse of a memory or interference from some other mind. Even I wasn't perfect. But it worked for the most part.

You two are kinda in trouble, I said. *I think the Gate has decided to kill you today. So, you know, you'd best make peace with your creator and stuff like that.*

Daniel didn't seem overly alarmed. I had to give him credit for that. *Why do they want to kill us?*

Don't take it personal. You and the Merry Men have messed up some of their minor plans here and there, and they're very put out.

I sensed he was running. Probably to alert Brenda. I felt the black-eyed peas converging. When out of range of my bubble of fuzzy real-ish vision, they looked like those clumps of wet rags. When they passed within the edge of my bubble, they looked like creepy elementary school band nerds. They neared, and I heard a doorbell ring somewhere.

Don't answer it, I said.

Another mind butted into the conversation. It was a presence I knew. Belinda, a.k.a., Smartmouth, a.k.a., Brenda. I knew she was brain shouting at me, but without prep and a couch and such, she couldn't do more than make a sound like squealing Styrofoam.

Ow, I said. *Kid, tell her to shut up. If she wants to say anything, have her tell you.*

Okay. He seemed a little less calm. *Who is at the door? Is it the people who want to kill us?*

It's your favorite lost children of doom, yes. They'll find a way in soon, but it's best not to just open the door for them.

A pause, and I sensed the black-eyed peas were almost through the door.

Brenda wants to know what we're supposed to do.

I sighed. *You're supposed to not go back to your home states in ones and twos so the Gate can pick you off easily. But I guess your little brain trust couldn't figure that one out. Why don't you tell her to offer to give 'em free tattoos and see if that works?*

A wave of hate enveloped me, and I knew the black-eyed peas had spotted me. I did a little thought shimmy to dodge their gaze. Despite their innocuous appearance as black-eyed children straight out of *The Addams Family*, these creatures were full-on evil. Imagine *The Exorcist* plus a banshee with a migraine.

Kid, listen to me very carefully. I can't be there to save you, and you don't have your little posse together to pool your meager talents, so you're going to have to work with Brenda and do what I say to get through this.

I felt the color of Brenda's thought change, which told me the kid had delivered my message. *We're ready,* he said.

Okay, good. Tell her to concentrate on getting angry at these things. She needs to get ticked off, kid. I'm talking about hellfire kind of anger. Righteous indig-freaking-nation. It's one of the few things that holds them off.

In the pause, Brenda's color temperature rose, and I could sense the black-eyes get shoved back. Which also had the effect of telling them exactly where she and Daniel were hiding. With the psychic snapshot she sent out, even *I* could see them in the coat closet.

The beasties were inside the house now and coming for them, and even Smartmouth didn't deserve to be torn limb from limb, and especially not by travel sized prep school rejects.

Kid, listen: You're the key here. I need you to do something you've probably never tried. I need you to create a fire with your mind. Not a real fire—a brain fire. Think of a torch or a—

In my mind's eye, I saw a flaming sword erupt in the night, like something out of *Legend of Zelda 25*. It was much larger than kid-sized. It was outlandishly huge, like something only animated characters could possibly wield. The flames looked real enough, like those on a very long burning torch, but thankfully they didn't seem to set anything on fire.

I saw Daniel's face illuminated in it. He looked scared but mad. Behind him stood Brenda trying to decide between protecting him and hiding behind him. I couldn't tell if she saw the sword. It didn't matter.

Before I could tell Daniel what to do, he kicked the closet door open and sliced down with the sword.

Five black-eyed school kids scattered back like cats scared by a cucumber. One fell and got up lamely. The sword was metaphysical only, but the metaphor must've held, because it seemed like metaphysical mutants could take damage.

The kid was good.

He strode to the kitchen in the false dark of my remote vision. The black-eyed freaks backed away, hissing like vampires in some stupid SyFy Channel show.

Behind you, kid!

He spun around, where two girl creatures had been sneaking up on him. He swung the sword and pulled Brenda behind him, and a blond girl mutant spun away without a metaphysical right hand.

You need to get the car keys, I told him. *Get in the car and go to the airport. I will have tickets waiting for you when you get there.*

Where are we—

I'm not going to tell you. Just do it.

I saw his visage shift color. *In case we're captured and tortured?*

Something like that. Now go.

I heard the Styrofoam again, and I knew Brenda was brain farting at me.

What does she want?

We can't, he said. *Her car's in the shop.*

Oh, right. *Figures. Okay, look, just go out front and find someone with a car. Go to the neighbors' or flag somebody down. I'll take care of it.*

Daniel swung the sword all around, keeping the black-eyed peas at bay as if he was a samurai warrior. They made a stand by the front door, but a swing from him and a surprising surge of righteous anger from Brenda, and the thing basically blew open.

Real-world lighting didn't look realistic through when I bilocated, so I couldn't see it, but I suspected Southern California sunlight was flooding the house now. Too bad it didn't make the beasties sparkle and die.

Daniel and Brenda went into the front yard. In the light of the sword, I could see a radius of only about ten feet.

What do you see, kid? Anyone getting in their car?

No, nobody— Oh, wait. I see Mr. Hernandez across the street.

I saw them step off the curb, but then Brenda pulled Daniel back so hard he almost dropped the sword.

Seriously, woman! What are you doing?

But into the spot where Daniel had just been

rolled the front of a giant brown panel van. A UPS truck. It screeched to a halt and the driver got out, colored afraid and angry, to see if they were all right.

Behind their little drama triangle, the black-eyed peas poured out of the house, and more joined them from the back yard. We didn't have time for Mr. Band-Aid.

Kid, say this to the driver. Say, 'What would you do if we borrowed your truck?'

Daniel asked the driver, and I got a mental image from the driver of what he would do. He would run after them and try to stop them. Shoot. I'd been hoping he'd just pull out his cell phone and call the police.

Okay, he's going to have to come along. Tell him there is a gang of scary arsonists trying to catch you and your...mom, and would he please get you to the police.

Daniel told him, and he looked at the black-eyed peas. He didn't seem inclined to action, but something changed—probably he saw those all-black eyes—and suddenly he was willing to receive suggestions.

Get in the van, Daniel. Tell Brenda to get in the passenger side and shut the door. If Mr. Driver gets in and drives, you're golden. If not, Brenda will have to learn how to drive a truck in a hurry.

I was going to walk them through the whole getaway bit, but other business nagged at me. I sensed that Tank—a.k.a., Cowboy, a.k.a., the troll—was about to have his innards handed to him, and I figured someone would be mad if I didn't at least make a token effort to save his skin too.

In my mind, I disengaged from the fun in SoCal and zoomed back out to the black nether with the encircling horizon of lights I might interact with. Sure enough, Tank had black fog sharks prowling near him too.

In a minute, in a minute. Everybody's so needy! What would they do without me? Seriously.

Even though I wouldn't want Sweet Cheeks mad at me if I didn't at least try to save him, I hated that being in the ether this long and this actively was going to reveal my location to…certain parties.

But what else could I do? I had to help Tank.

I needed to make a stop first. In that hypothetical space "above" the dark plane of my destinations was where the Watchers hung out. "Below" the plane was where the Gate had their icy fortress. Not going there today. This was taxing enough. So I bopped to the center of the black expanse and jetted up, pressing my mind at their ears.

The Watchers preferred talking and letting me pick up on their stuff, like a little psychic dog eating their crumbs. But I knew they also heard my thoughts. Our suite of rooms on the top floor of the DFW Grand Hyatt was proof of that. So I packaged my request into a little thought grenade and lobbed it up where I knew they were. Tickets, clearance at multiple airports, pack up their homes, create cover stories, along with a *Boom, make it happen* chaser. Then I was off to save the troll.

Chapter 2

THE TROLL

Tank was deep in fog.

I'd thought I'd find Tank the Troll Engine physically nearby Brenda and Daniel, since his pad was also in SoCal. But this wasn't L.A. Then I'd thought he was maybe with his uncle in Dicksonville, Oregon, playing junior detective again—assuming they could stitch two police uniform shirts together so it would fit him. But he wasn't there either.

I guess it didn't really matter where he was. What mattered was what floated around him in the pea soup he had gotten himself neck-deep into.

He was alone. Standing in the middle of a highway

ridged with rain forest. Standing beside a yellow road sign that said—what else?—FOG. Sure enough, there was fog here. All around him. Swirling and rising, floating like a ghost, shrouding like the edge of a dream.

And while Tank couldn't see the critters that swam around him, disturbing the mists and slavering for his flesh, I could see them fine. I'd read his memories about the San Diego debacle, of course, so I knew these were the same fog-sharks from before. Or their cousins. These were long snakes that had mouths like twenty fangs of death. Part lamprey eel, part severed tentacle, part chopped cucumber of biting—and all nightmare and murder.

At least with Daniel, I could communicate directly. Even Brenda could probably have heard me, if I'd pushed hard enough. How was I going to reach the captain of the Cro-Magnon wrestling team?

Then it hit me. I didn't know if I could do it, but if I didn't at least try, Sweet Cheeks would be mad at me. And if I *did* pull it off, she'd owe me. If you know what I mean.

I imagined myself heavy and agitated, which helped me climb out of my remote viewing trance. I found myself still sitting in the imperial suite of the Grand Hyatt at the DFW Airport. I was still surrounded by white fabric and silver chrome. I couldn't tell if the sun had moved, with the drapes closed, but I felt a little hungry, so some time must've passed. I was still propped up by plump pillows, so at least I hadn't fallen on my head and drooled on the fancy white carpet.

I scanned the room but didn't see what I wanted, so I went out into the living room-office area. There it was. I grabbed it from the desk and went back to the bed. Propped myself up, started the descent protocol again, and…sent a text.

Yo, Tank. Chad Thorton here. You're about to die. Get out of the fog.

I poised my finger over the Send button and jumped back into remote viewing—bilocating— mode. When I'd zoomed back over to Tank and his foggy bottom, I instructed my finger to press the button. Strange how much energy it took to make my body do anything when I was out of it.

Did he even have his phone with him? He was a Christian and therefore probably a Luddite, so it would figure if he'd left his—

I heard a beep that sounded suspiciously like a phone receiving a text.

But of course he didn't check his texts. His aura looked like he was close to wetting the bed, so getting an update about his favorite NFL team or a coupon from Troll-Mart probably wasn't high on his priority list.

Three lampreys coiled together like a Braided Missile of the Apocalypse and started bending in Tank's direction.

Troll, check your text, I thought at him.

No response. He spun around, though. Probably the lampreys had showed a hump of their back as they spiraled nearer.

Cowboy, check your phone. TANK, ya bonehead, I'm trying to save your red neck. Check that doohickey in the pocket of your Wranglers!

Nothing. But I did see his color change, and I think he was praying.

The death eels were sent tumbling outward as if hit

by a sonic detonation.

Yeah, that prayer stuff could be pretty useful sometimes. About ten times more effective than "righteous anger." He wasn't going to tell that to anyone, though.

Hey, person who thinks Andi would ever fall for him…get a clue and READ YOUR TEXT.

No response, and now the creatures were regrouping—angry, this time.

I bundled all my will into a thought and played my last card: *Bjorn Christiansen.*

His color shifted instantly blue, and I knew he'd heard me. He looked around in the fog as it drifted up to the lower branches of the evergreens around him.

I pushed my thought again. *Bjorn, you've got a very important text. Check it right now.*

He reached into his back pocket and pulled out his phone. A few swipes of his sasquatch thumb later, and I could see from his aura that he'd seen my text. The change in his posture suggested that he was trying to communicate with me telepathically, but that wasn't going to work.

I climbed out the bilocation and swiped another message.

Can c u but not ur thots. Drive out of fog NOW. San Diego monsters.

His color didn't change much when he read that one, so I thought he'd already figured out his danger. What he'd been doing wading through thick fog— next to a freaking permanent *fog* sign—after what he'd been through, was beyond even my brain's capacity.

Tank dug in his front pocket for his keys but dropped them. He bent down, and that was the opening the nearest death eel had evidently been waiting for. It darted forward, big as a kayak, and slammed Big Bjorn in the back of the neck.

I used my favorite German obscenity.

They went down in a pile of Scandinavian muscle and demon flesh. The troll was strong; I'll give him that. Even with an anaconda-sized monster on him, he fought for all he was worth. He got to his feet, gripping the thing hanging from the back of his neck in some kind of reverse stranglehold. The other eels smelled blood in the water and piled on.

German profanity.

I'd seen Andi's memories of that San Diego massacre, and I knew what generally happened when even one of these things attacked somebody. Generally…just a puff of pink mist and adios muchachos.

One thing was for sure: He wasn't going to be checking his texts anytime soon.

Well, Sweet Cheeks, no one can say I didn't try. Not that I was sad not to have a rival, but nobody deserved to die like—

The eels exploded off Tank like he'd erupted.

It even knocked me back, the wave of spiritual power that blasted off him.

The eel on his neck writhed and shivered like it was trying to get *away* from the guy but was hooked on by its circle of fangs. It stood out from Tank's body like a windsock in a tornado, until bits of it began flaying off. In a flash, it was only a skeleton flapping in the gale, and then even that disintegrated. Last of all, the mouth went to powder and poured away.

Holy bratwurst.

Tank struggled to his feet, blood pouring down the back of his neck onto his shirt. He put his hand back there and brought it forward to look at it. Red goop and lots of it. I was formulating an instruction burst for him, but he was ahead of me. He tore his shirt off and bound it around his neck to stanch the bleeding. I had to say that, even in a remote viewing of his torso, the shirt wasn't the only thing that was ripped.

I needed to be sure Andi didn't get to see him in a swimsuit until she was safely in my pocket.

The death eels were still in the area, swimming upstream against the reverse magnetism Tank was putting out. But unless he passed out from shock or blood loss, it didn't look like they were going to have another shot at him in the near future.

He staggered away from the forested hill he was on, leaving the FOG sign behind and moving toward his vehicle—an old Honda Civic from like 1832. No pickup—really?

The mists of bilocation obscured my vision and I thought I might lose touch with him. That happened sometimes. I heard the sound of a text message received, and I wondered who else might be sending him anything. Then I realized the text was on my end.

I rose from the RV trance and looked at my phone. It was from him.

Thx man.

I smiled in spite of myself. He was a dufus, but a plucky one.

Another message from him: *going 2 hsptal – heal didn't work* ☹

Good call. I wrote back. *Then take cab to airport. Tix waiting 4 u.* Wait, I had another thought. *wut is nearest airport 2 u?*

um... was his first text. Not helpful. Second was better: ***Del Norte, I think. crescent city, calif.***

k, thx

I put the phone down and went along the RV road again. One more little lamb to save before I could go to the hotel bar and collect a female companion for the evening. I had the very one in mind. There was a bartender named Ashley. Of course there was.

I didn't like the thought niggling my mind. But even if I didn't let myself fully think it, I couldn't escape the image of those creatures flung away from Tank like water off a dog.

That...that was power.

Ah, German profanity.

Never mind that. Now it was time to pay a little disembodied visit to my favorite pair of sweet cheeks.

A DAMSEL IN DISTRESS

It wasn't hard to locate Andi. I knew she had been planning to visit her grandparents at the beach house, and I'd seen her in transit a few days ago.

I hurried through the descent protocol and zoomed right to her. She was out with that black dog of hers, sitting on chaise lounge on the beach in her blue one-piece suit and with a book in her hands. That red hair rested on creamy white shoulders and contrasted beautifully with the cerulean swimsuit. It was sunny and bright, and beachcombers strolled by in the distance. No attack by evil nasties yet, but I knew from my quick journey here that they were moving in.

Funny how you can get to certain people faster, in remote viewing, when you've checked on them often.

Not that I've checked on her that much. Not saying that. Not saying that I've watched her journaling while sitting up in her bed. Not saying I've watched her fix meals for only herself in her apartment, chopping peppers and cooking stir-fry. Not saying I've learned her rhythms and gauged her aura. Definitely not saying I've been a little slow to pull away when she takes a shower.

Nope. Not saying any of that.

Hey, I'm not a stalker. At least, no one could bring charges.

It's just…she's interesting, that's all. Her mind is…nice. Orderly. Unexpected but always sensible. Even her whimsy is logical and delightful.

Besides, I couldn't be held responsible if, sometimes when I happened to check in on her, she wasn't entirely clothed. The vagaries of bilocating and all.

Andi, I thought at her. I hadn't tried this, and I didn't think she was gifted, but it was an experiment to see if intense feelings in the sender amplified the effects of the message. *Andi, can you hear me? It's Chad.*

Her aura permutated a bit and she put her book in her lap. She looked around, shading her eyes, as if thinking she'd heard someone call her name.

Good girl.

Then she made an *I must be hearing things* face and went back to her book.

I was reminded again that by now I had for sure flagged all the bad guys about where I was. *Hey, fellers, wanna come kill me?* Who knew what critters they were sending my way even now? Maybe they'd wait long enough for the whole club to convene at the hotel. Maybe they wouldn't.

Back to Sweet Cheeks. I was looking at her in a little, full-color holo-sphere in the middle of the black nether of remote viewing. Things were almost photorealistic in that bubble. But outside it, everything was symbolic and vague. Tiny lights and flitting clouds and waves of feeling, all churning together in the darkness.

But this wasn't my first rodeo, and I knew what was what. So when I again saw what appeared to be collections of gray rags billowing in the invisible breeze and roiling toward Andi like a wad of seaweed caught in the surf, I knew what they were.

This was not good. I knew without even checking that Sweet Cheeks wouldn't have her phone. She didn't like trying to use it in bright sunlight, and she wanted to unplug by the beach.

Not saying I'd studied her moods.

So…no texting her like I did Tank. And no direct communication like with Daniel.

Too bad my gifts weren't different. Then maybe I could hijack that dog of hers and start speaking through its mouth. Now that would be cool.

The balls of rag were closer now. In Sweet Cheeks' reality, they were probably already within a quarter mile of her. Maybe on the beach, maybe creeping up from the houses behind her, and maybe flying over the water. Maybe high above her or directly below.

What form would they take to get at her, I wondered. Tank's evil death eels? Black-eyed peas? Men in black with dark sunglasses over eyeless sockets?

I couldn't see much beyond the edge of the bubble. But it wouldn't matter for long. Soon enough, their chosen form would be all too clear.

Andi, you're in danger, I thought at her. *Andi, run!*

She put the book down again and cocked her head, but she didn't get up and flee.

I racked my prodigious brain for a solution. If I'd known about this earlier, I could've freaking called her and told her what was going on.

No, better: If they were all together in one place, as a team ought to be, none of this would've happened. They would've been grouped and could pool their pitiful resources. And when that didn't work, I could've saved them. But no, apparently they thought that fifty—or however many it had been—calls from the Watchers didn't suggest a pattern or imply that there might be fifty more. So these geniuses go back to their little sewing clubs and badminton teams or whatever and end up getting pounced on one by one. It was just a wonder it hadn't happened before now. Lucky for them, I was there now.

Except…what about my dear cheeks of sweetness? Was I going to have to watch that beautiful flesh torn apart before my eyes? Was that puzzling, delicious brain going to be seagull dinner surprise? If only I—

Right: the grandparents.

I started climbing out of the RV so I could look up their number, but I heard—felt, really—Andi's dog growl, and I knew it was show time.

The rag balls were near. Seven of them, at least. All I could see was Andi in her chaise lounge. Then a shadow fell over her. It was perfectly round.

Those shiny spheres. I'd seen them in action in

Vegas. I remembered how brave Stephie had been to take the gun and shoot at them. And even if that weren't true, I'd seen these things often enough in Andi's dreams to know what they were. Odd how they seemed to pick a different form for each member of the team. Wonder what they'd pick for me.

Andi's dog went into crazed attack mode, barking and snarling and snapping at the spheres—I could see some of the golden orbs in my periphery now—and then cowering away and yipping, as if under some dog-frequency assault.

Sweet Cheeks dropped her book and rolled to her feet, but there must've been other spheres behind her, because she stopped as if blocked.

I didn't like feeling helpless.

Chad?

The voice startled me worse than if a golden sphere had been right here in the hotel room with me.

"Who's that?" I asked the air.

It's Daniel. We're at the airport, but I know Andi's in trouble. I want to help.

Daniel! "You know what, Junior? You just might be able to help, at that." I let my brain run through the options. "Okay, look, I need to do what I can to protect Andi. You have Brenda use the airplane phone to call Andi's grandparents in Indian Rocks Beach. Tell them to call the police and an ambulance, because I'm afraid Andi's going to need them. Tell them to go out and find Andi on the beach and help her if they can."

Okay, but…Brenda says this plane doesn't have phones.

"Of course it doesn't. Okay, have her use her cell phone."

Um! We're not supposed to—

"Do it, kid! Screw the FAA. Andi's going to die."

I felt him thinking about it. *Okay.*

Brenda gave her psychic Styrofoam a twist, probably telling me off, but I didn't care, so long as she made the call.

"As for you, Daniel, you can absolutely help me. I've never tried this, but it might work. I almost got through to Andi a minute ago, alone. But with you and me shouting at her together, I think she might hear us. You up for it?"

Another thoughtful pause. *Well, yeah, but I can't see her. How will I know what to say?*

"I'll tell you, then we'll say it to her together. Got it?"

Okay.

I checked in with Andi.

She wasn't dead yet. That was good. But that might change soon. For some reason, she had run toward the water, not away from it. The orbs chased her like giant globular hornets. The dog stayed by her side, leaping at the things and falling hard back to the packed sand.

I caught a glimpse of people watching the spectacle. Not surprisingly, they were dumbfounded. Dumb something else, if you'd asked me.

A couple of slobby surfers ran to Andi's rescue, jabbing their boards at the things like wide poles. One took a wide roundhouse swipe at an orb and slammed it on the side.

It recoiled from the blow and knocked into the sphere next to it, and I had an insane inner vision of pendulum balls merrily smacking into one another. But the two affected balls arrested themselves in the air, made an aggressive move toward the surfers, and then *boom*, the dudes went flying away, feet sailing over their heads.

Gnarly wipeout, dude. Cha.

I couldn't see them, but I sensed that Andi's grandparents were on the case now. I suspected they were on their way over the dunes toward her. Probably both would have heart attacks on the way.

Meanwhile, the spheres were still buzzing Sweet Cheeks and Wonder-Dog.

Why did the balls of gray rags use the metal orb devices? Part physical conveyance, I knew, but what was scary about shiny cue balls? Still, anyone who knew Andi's dreams like I did would know that it was a good form for them to use against her.

People were fleeing the scene now, and nobody else offered to help. The surfers were limping away with their boards.

An orb dipped too low, and the dog jumped at it, maw open. Not sure what it had in mind, but I couldn't fault its devotion. The sphere sent out a beam of some kind, and I felt the dog's pain across the ether. It fell to the sand in a broken heap, like a deer hit by a truck.

"Abby!" Andi looked at her dog in shock, maybe waiting for it to move. Then she fell to her knees beside it and pulled its head into her lap. I could see her sobbing. The spheres closed in, and things were going to be over very, very quickly.

Kid, I thought at Daniel, *I need you to say this with me. Say, 'Andi, you can't stay there. Get up and run.' You ready?*

I'm ready, Chad.

And…now.

Together, we said, ***Andi, you can't stay there.***

Get up and run.

She looked up suddenly, and I knew she'd heard us. "Is someone there?"

Kid, I said, *say, 'Your grandparents are in danger. They need your help.' And…now.*

Your grandparents are in danger. They need your help.

They weren't really in danger, yet, but I figured it would take something like that to get her off her sweet cheeks and into motion.

Andi looked to her left, toward the beach houses. "Sabba? Safta?" Abruptly, she stood, and I figured she'd spotted her grandparents. She ran toward them, and the orbs gave way.

I heard a squeal of Styrofoam, and I knew what that meant.

Brenda wants to help, Daniel said.

No kidding. I sighed. *Look, I don't have time to… Okay, fine, she can do this: Tap her whenever we're brain-shouting at Andi. Have her join her righteous fury—or her angry eyes or whatever she can bring—to what we're saying. Okay? Tell her, but hurry up.*

After a second, he said they were ready.

Back on the beach, Andi had reached two old people I knew from her memories were her rich grandparents. They looked terrified. Money's nice, but it can't save you from demon balls in the sky, you know what I'm saying?

I figured we had another five minutes before the police got there, unless we got lucky and a car was already in the area. So, now that we had a way to communicate with Sweet Cheeks, what was my plan going to be—hide behind Granny?

As the spheres converged on Andi and her

grandparents, I saw in my mind's eye an image of the death eels blasting off Tank back in the rain forest. I didn't like the plan that my usually reliable brain began to tell me about.

Um, Andi, I said, knowing she couldn't hear me without my helper, but just trying the idea on for size, *how do you feel about praying?*

I was aware of Daniel in the mindspace around me. *You want me to say that, too?*

No! Well, I mean…what do you think?

I dunno. It works like almost all the time. Against our bad guys, I mean.

Based on my observations, he was right. But that didn't mean I had to admit it. *I dunno, kid. How about we just have her run into the house until the cops get there?*

I could almost imagine Daniel making a wry face. *You think she's got time?*

Not for a minute. *How about we get her to whip up some of that 'righteous indignation' stuff you guys used?*

I dunno. Okay.

I looked in on Andi, and it seemed like she was up to something. She had picked up a hefty driftwood log and was brandishing it like a baseball bat. Moms and Pops backpedaled behind her. Andi seemed to be tracking one certain orb amidst the swarm of balls crossing and floating and throwing their shadows over her. The one she tracked seemed to stay back from her more than the others did.

She'd seen a pattern.

I shook my head. She was a wonder, that one.

Sweet Cheeks hefted the log and stepped backward. Their melee had brought them all the way to the back deck of her grandparents' house. Andi stepped up on it and retreated from the steps. Judging from how her eyes darted to the ground and the orbs, and the calculating look on her face, she was about to do something really brave. Or stupid.

The spheres moved over the deck too, perhaps anticipating that their prey was planning to go inside. One of them darted forward and struck Grams in the shoulder. She went down like a carpet bag, and Gramps bent to catch her.

That's when Andi struck. She sidestepped one orb, leapt forward on the deck, and brought the log crashing right into the face of the sphere she'd been watching.

A knot in the log cracked the golden carapace. A gust of black smoke lit by orange sparks flew out, and the orb lost altitude like a wounded quail. The other orbs hesitated and rose to a stationary orbit ten feet above the deck as if going into some kind of standby mode.

Andi chased the cracked orb off the deck, pounding on it like a woodsman going after a rattlesnake. It dodged and rolled and tried to gain altitude, but a well-placed smack on the top and it fell to the sand lifelessly. She beat it and beat it and beat it some more. I could see she was crying.

Chad, Daniel said, shocking me out of my trance, *what's happening? It feels like she's doing better.*

I nodded. *Yeah, she is. We may not have to use the crutch after all. Can't say I'm sorry. She went all Jolly Green Giant on the queen orb, and the rest don't know what to do.*

Andi ascended the steps of the deck like Abraham Lincoln, Vampire Slayer, and checked on Grams. She looked okay.

Okay, kid, I thought at him, *say this with me. 'Good job, but they won't be out long. Get everybody inside.' Ready?*

Go.

Good job, but they won't be out long. Get everybody inside.

Andi dropped the log and opened the door to the house. She pulled Gramps and Grams toward it just as the orbs lowered ominously. One moved to behind the other ones, and if I could see which one was the new queen, Sweet Cheeks sure could.

The two front spheres floated "shoulder to shoulder" and fired a beam that splintered the beach house wall, showering them with kindling.

Andi and her grandparents fell backward into the house and crab-walked away. A third orb joined the line and I could tell they were about to fire again.

Andi!

The leftmost orb shattered and fell.

Black smoke billowed from somewhere, and I registered the blast of a large-barreled weapon. The spheres turned their attention to the newcomer, but two more of them popped like fog balloons. The new queen went down next, its casing caved in.

I saw the four policemen then. Three fired 9mm handguns, but the fourth—a strapping, young, leading man sort of hero—had a pump-action shotgun the likes of which I'd last seen in a zombie apocalypse movie.

The other orbs went into standby mode again, which just made it easier for the Terminator to send them all to the shiny sphere afterlife.

I sighed. With that done, there would be much talkety-talk and the filling out of reports: The detectives-with-notepads sort of scenes you see on every TV police drama. Then the Watchers would send their clean-up crew with their hush money and special "incentives" to make it all go away. The worst of it was that, for the next hour or so at least, my Sweet Cheeks would be all beholden to Police Prince Charming, and I wouldn't even be on her mind.

Kid, I need you to say one more thing with me.

Is Andi okay?

She's fine. Better than fine. I thought again of Ashley the bartender. Did she have a pretty friend? I was going to need a double dose after this.

What do you want me to say with you?

Say, "You did good, Sweet Cheeks. As soon as you can, get to the airport. There will be a ticket." Ready?

Uh, I don't want to call her "Sweet Cheeks."

I smiled in spite of myself. *Okay, we'll call her "Andi." And…whoa, wait.*

As I watched, Andi jumped from the deck and ran for the beach. The police called after her, but I knew where she was going. The dog.

Hang on a sec, I thought at Daniel.

She sprinted and I could see the tears flying down her cheeks. Andi shooed away a gaggle of seagulls and crabs and fell beside the black mass on the sand. The tide was coming in, and at that moment the edge of a wave came nearly to where they lay. She was crying from fear and shock and everything else, I knew, but mainly for the loss of her old friend, one who had died trying to protect her.

It was an unselfish love that felt so pure as to be out of my reach. A love only saints and St. Bernards were capable of.

Without permission, a thought of Stephie exploded in my mind. Poor Stephie, my erstwhile assistant in Las Vegas who had helped me master remote viewing. Who had endured my abuse and loved me anyway. Who had taken freaking demons off my soul and onto hers, and had then run into traffic.

I stared at the black landscape of soul travel and felt...

Dead.

I didn't know how many times Daniel had called my name before I finally heard it. *Chad?*

I put away the memories of Stephie. A lot of thoughts I didn't like had come to me today. I put them all away.

Yeah, kid?

Are we going to say that thing to Andi now? I'm afraid I'm going to forget it.

I felt a smile stretch my cheeks. *Sure. Ready...go.*

You did good, Andi, we said together. **As soon as you can, get to the airport. There will be a ticket.**

There's no "camera" in remote viewing. My observing presence is everywhere and nowhere specific at the same time. But when Andi heard our message, I could swear she looked right at me. She raised her head from Abby and gave me a sad smile that I didn't have to be psychic to understand meant *Thank you.*

Chapter 4

TO THE SWEET SUITE, TOUT SUITE

I greeted them standing up.

Ashley sat in elegant repose on the smart gray couch in the living room portion of my entertaining area, and I stood behind her like a Mexican don with his expensive mistress.

The four of them schlepped in like wet cats pulled from the sewer. The bellhop let them in and stood aside.

Brenda looked more dour than usual. She stepped onto the brown parquet floor, looked over my entertainment area from left to right, and dropped her purse with a fake leather splat.

Tank managed to be taller than I remembered from Vegas, and even hunched from fatigue and the pain from that bandaged wound on the back of his neck, he still looked like he might have to duck through the doorway. His eyes widened at all the white and gray and chrome, and probably at the expanse of windows looking out over the DFW runways. But when the troll's gaze rested on Ashley, I saw that trademark Christian disapproval, and once again, it didn't take superpowers to see what he thought was going on between us.

Sweet Cheeks looked radiant, despite her weariness and the fact that she wore more clothes than I preferred. She'd put that glorious red hair into a quick ponytail—how often I'd seen her do it in just three graceful moves. She wore a brown blouse and khaki capris and brown leather sandals that clapped on the parquet. But her eyes were sad, and something in me lurched.

Daniel was the only one who seemed mostly unchanged. He stepped into the room, spun around to take it all in, then sat next to Ashley on the couch and picked up the TV remote.

"Hi," Ashley said to him.

He gave her a quick smile. "Hi."

I spread my arms magnanimously. "Welcome to Fantasy Island."

They looked at me without comprehension.

"Oh, come on," I said, dropping my arms. "None of you has watched old reruns of that show? Ricardo Montalban? Tattoo? 'Boss! Da plane! Da plane!' Nothing? Seriously? Wow, you guys are missing out."

Brenda trudged over to the white chair beside the couch and flopped into it. "Only thing I'm missing is a bed. You got one in this place, pretty boy, or imma gonna sleep right here?"

The others surged in, as well. Tank took a spot beside Daniel on the couch, all but launching Daniel and Ashley in the air when he sat.

"Please, sit," I said. "We have a moment before dinner."

The troll roused at that. "Dinner?"

"Of course."

Andi rounded the coffee table and came to the matching white chair at the other end of the couch. Before sitting, she met my eyes and gave a fleeting smile. When she sat, she looked forward in the chair and saw something no one else had remarked about. "Ooh, an aquarium!"

Inset in the wall and beside the doorway they'd all entered through was a blue-tinted aquarium the size of a small walk-in bath. Small and medium-sized fish and crabs and other critters circled around in their eternal aquatic boredom. Still, it was nice to look at. And I didn't have to maintain it, so it was a win.

I took a moment to read their thoughts. Mostly they were tired and upset with me for presuming to bring them here—"He ain't the boss of me!" was how Smartmouth was thinking it—and still shaken from their ordeals.

It really wasn't fair, my ability to hear thoughts before, during, and after a discussion with people. Too bad. Fair was for losers.

And with what was going to happen to them tonight, they ought to be extra glad of my gift. I took a sniff of the ether around me and felt sure I knew what had been sent—or drawn—here because of my prolonged time in RV.

I remembered the encounter in Chile all too clearly.

I stifled the ghastly thought and looked down at Ashley. She was gorgeous, dear thing, as all female bartenders should be. Long, dark brown hair now swept across her right shoulder. Beautiful smile and tasty lips. Trim figure, of course, and the palest porcelain skin. She still wore the powder blue button-up shirt and black slacks she'd worn at the bar, and she smelled faintly of wine. But she was an excellent couch decoration and had been—and would continue to be—a delightful companion when other options weren't presenting themselves.

I knelt beside her. "Ash, be a doll and go check on our dinner, won't you, hmm? Our guests are famished."

"Of course," she said. I sensed a bit of upset about being dismissed, but I knew she was into me. She patted my cheek and left the suite.

"Who's that?" Brenda asked. "Your new Stephie? Gotta have one on your arm at all times, playa?"

I ignored her and sat in the spot still warmed by Ashley's pretty backside. "First," I said to all of them, "you're welcome. You know, for saving your lives."

Brenda gave me an *are you serious?* look. "Unbelievable."

I smiled. "Any of the rest of you want to deny it?"

Tank's hand went up to the back of his neck. "So like, how did you know, you know? How'd you know that was going to happen?"

I tapped my temple. "But I didn't have to have the gift to see that one coming. You dolts punch the Gate in the nose and then walk off alone, la-de-da. Might as well wrap yourself in bacon and jump in the lion pen."

"Yeah," Tank said, "but nothing like that's ever happened before, and we've done this a dozen times or more."

"I know you have. And you're just lucky they didn't try it before I was there to save your sorry butts." I turned to Andi. "Except yours isn't sorry, Sweet Cheeks."

She stood and slapped my face.

"Ow!" My cheek stung, but what was worse was that I hadn't seen it coming.

She brought a finger into my face. "That's for being crass."

"That's what I'm talkin' about," Brenda said, giving Andi a high five.

"And there's another one of those for you every time you're crass in the future."

As the sting faded from my face, my admiration rose. Not only could I not figure her out yet, she could surprise me. That was a big deal for mind readers.

"But," Andi said, settling back in her chair, "I do wonder how you knew we were in trouble."

I worked my jaw. "Well, somebody has to look out for your sorry...um, selves. As soon as Moose here got on the plane in Vegas, I came here and started making arrangements. This is your new home now. And I looked in on—"

"Whoa," Daniel said, looking interested for the first time. "We're living *here?* Cool! Can I have a room with an aquarium too?"

Everyone started talking at once. That, plus all their jumbled thoughts, was a lot to sort through. But by now I knew how to endure it. I brought up mental shields, sent my mind to a happy place—which might or might not have included Andi's room—and waited it out.

"No," Brenda finally said. "Nobody's movin' nowhere, no how. Mm-um. I gots bills to pay."

I shook my head. "Not anymore, you don't."

That shut them all up.

"What's that supposed to mean?" Sweet Ch— Um, Andi asked.

"It means," I said, standing and walking behind the couch, my arms sweeping the suite, "that we five, we merry five, are the permanent and sole residents of this entire end of the top floor of the DFW Grand Hyatt. You each have a suite to yourself. Not as nice as this one. This one's mine. But a suite almost as large. Belinda and Daniel—"

"Brenda," Smartmouth corrected.

"—have a two-room executive suite right next door. You, Cowboy-Tank, have a presidential suite, and you, Andi, their finest bridal suite."

They were ridiculously easy to read. And to placate, apparently.

"This," I said, looking around the room where we all were, "will be our headquarters. Except, of course, when I have guests and need my privacy."

Brenda harrumphed. "So, basically, we can't be in here, ever."

I let it go. But she wasn't wrong.

"Wait," Andi said, "let's go back to the part about how this is now our home. That's not going to work for me. I've got to get back to Florida. I've got a—"

"What?" I asked. "You've got a what? An apartment in Cambridge near the university where you worked with the Professor. Except wait, the

Professor went body surfing in the nether, didn't he? Which means you're not working with him, which means you don't have a job at the university, which means you don't need to be in Cambridge. Or in Indian Rocks Beach, with your grandparents, as you were about to say next."

Andi opened her mouth and quickly closed it.

I loved being psychic.

"I'm sorry about your Gram-Gram, but she'll be all right. As will Grampa Willy, and their house. They've now been told that those flying orbs were a NASA experiment gone wrong and that you've been offered a prestigious job in a secret facility somewhere and won't be allowed to come back for long stretches at a time." Then something came over me and I felt blue. I didn't like blue. "I am sorry about Abby, though. She was…"

And suddenly I was close to weeping. Me! I shut it down hard.

"As for you," I said to Brenda, "your 'body art' business has, as far as anyone knows, been bought out by a local real estate investor and converted into a Buddhist temple."

"What?"

"No, I don't actually know what they'll put there. I just wanted to see your reaction."

She told me, both verbally and mentally, what she thought of me. Funny girl.

"Oh," I said, "it's also dumb that you're just sort of the kid's guardian. I mean, what does that even mean? So I got that noise all fixed. He's yours now."

"What?" they all said.

"What-what? The adoption. It's finalized. Well, the papers need your final sig. They're over there on the desk." I looked seriously at Daniel. "I know it's a lot of responsibility, Daniel. So are you really sure you want to adopt this girl? She's kind of a wild child."

He giggled and looked at Brenda.

She wanted to object, I knew, but why? Instead, she smiled and called Daniel into a huge hug.

Yeah, that felt pretty good, I guess. And I wasn't done handing out goodies. Santa had something for one and all.

Besides, you kinda have to keep the person happy who knows your deepest hurts from the past. A happy holder of secrets is a quiet holder of secrets. Or so I hoped.

"How are you doing all this, Chad?" Andi asked.

"Oh, it's not me." I pointed upward. "It's them."

Tank leaned forward. "Angels?"

"No," I said, chuckling. "*Them*. The Watchers. But I guess small minds could think of them as angels. It wouldn't be the first time."

"So, what…" Tank said, and I knew he was smarting from the put-down… "you just send 'em a memo and they say, 'Yes, sir, Chad, sir!' Is that how it goes?"

"Now, now, Cowboy. Maybe he knows a few things we don't." She gave Daniel a squeeze, and I knew she had become a semi-ally, at least for now.

At that moment, there came the sound of a key card in the door to my suite, and the door swung open. Ashley came in and held the door open for a Hispanic waiter pushing a silver cart with silver domes. The dishes clinked and rattled as he drove the wheels over the metal threshold.

I watched this one carefully as they came in. I knew what he was, of course. I'd grappled with them

41

in Chile a few months back. Well, I hadn't been physically there, but it was the same difference. I didn't know yet what this one was planning, and its thoughts were hidden from me. He was too early, but it wasn't as if they were exactly under my control.

We were all in deadly danger.

A SENSIBLE CHANGE

"Your dinner tonight," Ashley said as the waiter lifted the domes, revealing piles of fancy entrees on oversized dish-bowls, and began arraying the dining table, "is Atlantic halibut, braised artichoke, carrot, fava, and confit tomato, with a lemon and Thai basil sauce." She swept her hand over the table. "Please, come sit."

When the waiter took food, not automatic weapons, from under the domes, I figured we were okay at least for a while longer.

I went to Ashley and gave her a kiss on the lips—an act that surprised but thrilled her, I perceived. But it got no strong reaction from Andi, so it was mostly wasted effort. "Thanks, Ash. This is great. Will I...see you later tonight?"

She tucked her hair behind her ear and smiled without looking at me. "You know where to find me."

"I sure do."

"I'm off at midnight."

"Oh, please," Brenda said, pulling a chair out from the table, "get a room. Wait…I guess you did."

"Good night, all of you," Ashley said. "Enjoy your dinner." She followed the waiter and his trolley out of the room and into the hallway.

The dining table and chairs sat on a square, blue and white throw rug, which looked nice and presumably kept the chair legs from scratching the parquet.

They tore into their food. I cut a piece of halibut and stuck it on my fork.

Tank made a big show of praying first, but then he dug in too. "So, Chad," he said, "save us the trouble. Tell us what you've done. All this." He twirled his fork in the air.

"Well, I could. I could tell you everything, then you'll all tell me why it won't work and how you've got other plans. Then I'll ask Andi to tell us the pattern she's already seen, and then I'll ask Belinda to whip out her sketch book and show us the sketches she's already made of her room here and…a creepy ghast dude I'll explain about later. And finally you'll all agree that I was right." I ate my bite of halibut. "So can we please just skip to that part and enjoy our dinner? There's crème brûlée in the fridge."

They sat there deciding what to say. Then Daniel belched—"Sorry"—and the tension broke.

"You still haven't told us what all you've done,"

Andi said, sipping sweet tea. "I'd like to hear it."

I took a big breath. "Okay, let's see. First, it's beyond stupid that you guys aren't living together, but I've already covered that. And now you have a headquarters for your Mystery, Inc. clubhouse, and I'm working on a Mystery Machine for us too. What say, Scoob," I said to Tank, "you be the dog and I'll be Shaggy? She's Daphne," I said, looking at Andi, "she's Velma," to Brenda, "and you, kid, can be Fred."

Daniel blinked at me. "I have no idea what you're talking about."

"Never mind. So, now you're all together, as you should've been from the beginning."

Brenda started to speak, but I shushed her.

"Andi," I said, but what I thought was *Sweet Cheeks,* "please tell them the pattern you've seen."

She looked like she'd just been asked to narc on her best friend. She swallowed her tea and set the glass down carefully. "Well, it does seem like the four of us—maybe the five of us now—are being called on again and again. And unless you all haven't been telling me everything, we're not doing other missions on our own or with other groups, right?"

"Right," Tank and Brenda said. How much better they responded to Andi than to me. Would that change over time?

"So if the trend continues," Andi said, "it would mean we will continue to be called upon to come together to meet whatever need arises."

"Until Jesus comes!" the troll said.

"Rrrright," Andi said. "And it does make a certain amount of sense for us to be together so we can respond more quickly, instead of having to first get on planes to reassemble and then fly out again. And," she said with a reluctant look at me, "though I don't relish the thought of living in Texas, I can't argue with the logic of being near a major international airport. Plus, I've seen today that our being with our loved ones puts them in danger." She sighed as if having to deliver bad news to good people. "Yeah, so, I guess an arrangement like this is actually pretty smart. And…the food's good."

This time it was Tank's turn to belch. "No doubt. But do you think they make cheeseburgers?" He wiped his mouth. "Seriously, though, I basically have no reason to live in California. No reason to live in any specific spot, you know? If I'm not going to be a sheriff's deputy in Dicksonville, and I'm not, I might as well live in Texas, where I grew up, y'all. Plus, Dallas Cowboys Stadium is *right here*." He leaned back and met all their eyes, but his gaze lingered on Sweet Cheeks. "You all are my family now. My team. Of course I want to stick with you. Besides, these digs do beat my roach-trap one bed/one bath, you know?"

"Excellent, Bjorn," I said.

He made a face. "'Tank,' please."

Troll. "Right, 'Tank.'"

"What's mine?" he asked.

"I'm sorry?"

"What's my cover story? Did you tell my uncle and all?"

"Oh, right. Anyone who might be curious has been or will be told that you are doing private bodyguard work for executives and a lucrative firm and won't be reachable for months at a time."

He looked like he'd just won a calf roping contest. "A bodyguard? Woohoo! Look out, ladies, I'm your

James Bond security detail for the evening."

Brenda cooed and swiveled her shoulders. "I declare, I feel safer already!"

"Chad," Andi asked me, "what about our apartments and such?"

"It's all taken care of. Your belongings are being shipped here as we speak."

Brenda scratched her head. "Hey, I still owe—"

"All your debts have been paid."

A stunned silence. Even Tank stopped eating.

"You guys are such amateurs," I said. "Do you really think I would forget anything?" I felt Daniel looking at me meaningfully, so I turned an ear to his thoughts.

What will we do for money?

"Good question," I replied aloud. "Some of you may be wondering what you'll do for money if you have no job and you disappear from the face of the earth. Not to worry—your Uncle Chadley has taken care of it. For the larger things, like room and board and jetting off to who knows where, that's all being handled by a higher power. No, Tank, not God or angels, but you can think of it that way if it helps."

He didn't like that one either. I was going to have to tone it down around him for a while. "As for spending money, you've each got a monthly allowance of five thousand dollars and no expenses. So...live it up."

I went to the midsize fridge in the little kitchenette beside us and pulled out the tray of crème brûlée.

Brenda looked doubtfully at the fancy little bowl I put before her. "What's the catch?"

"No catch!" I said. "No catch! You're all doing a job here. An important one, even if you're not as skilled as me, at least you've got some ability. I saw that in you this morning. The powers that be seem to think you're useful together, so this, all this, is just you being together. Seriously, what's your problem? Somebody wants to give you tons of money and bring you to live in luxury and do important work, and you're hesitating?

"You know what? Fine. Go on back to your tattoo parlor, Brenda. Why not? Go back into debt. Then act all surprised when you get called up to another mission and have to hoof it to the airport and come here and get on another plane and fly wherever. Live in squalor, sure. And you haven't signed those papers, so Daniel isn't really yours. I can make that go away in a hurry. That's what you want, I guess."

I was standing, but I didn't remember getting up. "What about the rest of you? Wanna go back to your lonely spots and get picked off one by one? Go right ahead. Anyway, Brutus," I said to Tank, "what in the name of Napoleon's sphincter were you doing all alone out in the middle of a foggy forest? You got a death wish, is that it?"

"No! I didn't think—"

"Of course you didn't. None of you do. If you didn't have me, all of you would be dead right now. So you're welcome. Excuse me for trying to make things smarter, do things better, take care of your needs, and keep you safe. Now go on out and die in the street. Go on, leave."

Nobody moved. Their thoughts were right there for the taking, but I didn't feel like hearing them. So I just stood there staring at the fools and thinking uncontrollably about Stephie and the sound she'd made when those creatures had entered her mouth.

At length, Daniel cracked his dessert with a spoon and had a taste. I could tell he liked it. Tank consumed his in four bites flat. Andi only picked at hers.

Brenda didn't even try it. "Don't take this the wrong way," she said. "I mean, you guys are great. But I like my space. I kinda like seeing you characters once and awhile and then going back to my own place, my own world. You know, ink and needles and home-schooling this kid. But…"

"Me, I'm all for it," Tank said. "Count me in, and grateful. Brenda, you gonna eat that?"

She slid the bowl to him and he attacked it.

"Chad," Andi said, and I melted at the sound, "I have a question."

I sat. "Give it to me, baby."

"How did you arrange all this? I mean, we were all with you in Las Vegas not that long ago. And where did the money come from? I can't imagine how much it had to cost to buy out this suite for just one night, much less have multiple premium suites indefinitely. Plus the way you say our homes have been cleaned out and our debts paid off—thank you for that, by the way—and the cover stories and all. How did you manage it?"

I could look into those green eyes forever. I could've saved her the effort of saying all that, of course, having heard it from her brain already. But why would I miss the chance to have that visage turned upon me for that long and to hear those dulcet tones?

I sighed contentedly. "I only asked for it, Andi. You guys had access to this all along, but I guess none of you thought to ask. Or did you think all the international plane tickets they kept sending you were emptying their piggy bank?" I shook my head disdainfully, but out of respect for Sweet Cheeks managed not to say, *Idiots*.

Brenda stood and walked to the desk. She picked up the pen and looked at the adoption documents. Everyone else watched her, but I didn't need to. I knew what she had decided. In a moment, I heard the pen scribbling on the paper. I figured there would ensue much hugging and blubbering among them, but she surprised me by touching my shoulder.

"Thank you, Chad." Though she blinked under the effort, Brenda nevertheless held my gaze. "I owe you." She laid two crumpled sheets of notepad paper on the table before me. The one on top showed her bedroom and the view out the window. "I'd like to see this place now, if that would be okay."

"Yeah," I said, my voice raspy despite myself. "Yeah, okay." I stood to lead her to their suite, but then the hugging and blubbering did commence, so I sat back down and looked at the second sheet of paper.

It was a drawing of a female ghast. It looked similar to the one I tangled with in Chile. When showing their true form, ghasts manifested as frighteningly emaciated figures with very long, thin limbs and a penchant for formalwear and gaudy jewelry. They did have facial features, but their faces were obscenely old and wizened, and their eyes were orbs of pure white. To use modern cultural terms, they were the halfway point between Slenderman and Tolkien's barrow wights.

And the hotel was crawling with them.

WHO YA GONNA CALL?

"Could I have your attention, please?" I said.

Mystery, Inc. had moved back to the couch and were in a completely different mood than what they'd been in when they'd first stepped in. Now they acted like lucky lottery winners just starting to spend their money. They looked at ease in this posh white and chrome suite, and I knew without reading anyone's mind that I had won them over.

Tank shushed them all. "Yeah, Chad, whatcha got, brah?"

"Thanks, Tank," I said, because I needed them to listen. "None of you have brought up the only major concern about us living together and always coming back to one home base."

Brenda harrumphed. "You mean that we'll figure out we don't really like each other? That this is a cage, even if it's coated in gold? That living in a hotel isn't the same as having a home? Am I getting close?"

"Not remotely." I looked at Daniel and raised an eyebrow. I thought *Do you know?* at him, but I knew he couldn't hear me if we weren't bilocating.

But maybe he read my face, because he nodded and pulled away from Brenda's embrace. "It makes us easy to find."

That sent a chill through the room. Only the fish seemed unaffected.

"Are you saying we're in danger here?" Andi was again in the chair where she'd first sat. Funny how people do that.

"We're in danger everywhere we go, Sweet…Andi. I was marked by the Gate years ago, and now even you lot are on their radar. The question isn't whether or not you're in danger, but whether you're in more danger alone or when together."

"Probably more together," Smartmouth said, pulling Daniel back to her. "Now they don't even have to look for us."

I chuckled. "Newsflash, Belinda, but they've never had to look for you. Here, at least, together, we can help each other out." I pulled from my pocket the second sketch Brenda had handed me and smoothed it out on the coffee table in front of the sofa.

They gathered around it. All but Brenda, who looked at me darkly.

"Huh," Tank said. "Looks like a creepy Aunt Skinny."

"What is it?" Brenda asked.

"They're called *ghasts*. Real stinkers, they are."

Daniel sat cross-legged on the parquet. "They're already here, aren't they?"

Everyone spun on him. "Say what?"

"Yup," I said, putting my hands in my pockets. "I've sensed three."

"Where?" Andi said. "Here? In the hotel?"

"Yup. Thanks to how I had to stay bilocated for so long today, it hung a target on my back and drew them here. In fact," I said with a nod to the hallway leading to the front door, "one of them has already been in this room, while you were here."

Now they spun on me. "What? When?"

"It was that bartender girl, wasn't it?" Tank asked. "I knew she was bad news."

"Listen, Moose, just because you don't approve of someone's morals doesn't mean they're minions of the Gate. For your information, no, it wasn't Ashley. It was the waiter."

Andi's mouth dropped open, but it was Brenda who spoke. "You trippin'. He didn't look nothin' like what I drew."

"They don't manifest in that form, Belinda. Not until they're about to strike. They look like normal peeps the rest of the time."

Tank surprised me by shuddering. "Guys, he was right here."

It occurred to me that having these ghasts here might actually help me prove my point to these simpletons. If we could come together, with or without a round of "Kumbaya," and toss out a few minor stink-bugs, my case would be made that much stronger. This could be perfect.

"Right," I said. "Okay, fine. So here's the thing: There are three ghasts here in the hotel. They've been sent by the Gate to kill us. They think we don't know what they are, since you at least haven't encountered them before. Plus I think they're just sort of throwing together a token attack, now that they've seen we're together. But they're dangerous, even alone, and we've got three. And we," I said, holding my arms out like Ricardo Montalban again, "are going to find and defeat them."

Brenda wagged her head. "Do what now?"

I walked to the couch, scooted Tank aside, and sat on the middle cushion. "You guys are such noobs. All this time you've been working together, but it's like you're making things up on the spot every time. It's time you started thinking strategically and tactically about how to use your abilities, lame as they are, and work as a team." I pulled my legs up, yogi-style. "I'm going to sit here and lead, and you Scooby Snacks are going to go find the nasties and send them packing."

Oh, how I did love getting that look of disbelief from them. This was going to be fun.

"Excuse me?" Brenda said, but that's all she had.

"You know," Tank said, "when I was playing football, the team leader led from the field, not the sidelines or the locker room…or the armchair."

"That's because when you were playing football, the quarterback wasn't psychic. So here's how it's going to work. I'm going into remote viewing to locate the ghasts. Then you're—"

"Can you do that from here, Chad?" Andi asked. "Without your couch and…"

She was really kind, wasn't she? "And without Stephie? Yeah, I can. Remember, it was only this morning that I did this with all of you guys. I sat on my bed," I thumbed behind to the left, toward my bedroom door, "and found you out there in those dangerously alone places you all were. Besides, we have our phones."

Tank brought his out of his pocket and grinned at it stupidly. "Oh, right."

What we really ought to have was professional comm units, I realized. So I sent a mental note up to the Watchers for next time and started slowing my breathing while I talked. "You will not break up into pairs, like they do on Scooby Doo. You will all travel together." I thought for a minute. I wanted Andi as far from Cowboy's ripped abs as I could put them. "Moose will go first, as cannon fodder, followed by Daniel, then Belinda and Andi."

"Brenda."

"And it's 'Tank.'"

"Whatever. You will go where I tell you, and when you encounter a ghost, you will each deploy the weapons I saw you use this morning."

They looked at each other.

"What weapons?" Tank asked.

I snickered. "Really? Vunderkind here," I said, looking at Daniel, "wielded a metaphysical sword of fire just a few hours ago. We'll need it again, kid. Swing it at the creatures like you did in the kitchen, okay? Belinda attacks with ink needles and sketchbooks, and occasionally her 'righteous anger' even has a small effect on things. I'll need you to be broadcasting that anger against all things creepy pretty much the whole time you're out," I told her. "It's like your shields."

"What about me?" Tank asked. "What's my secret weapon?"

"You will stand ready to bash in the heads of

anything that tries to attack Sweet Cheeks or the kid."

"Hey!" Andi said.

"Yeah," Brenda echoed. "What about me?"

I shrugged but gave her a roguish smile. "Moose," I said to Tank, "you've got some small but fritzy talent to heal. Hopefully you won't need it, because I expect none of you to be hurt and I definitely don't want any civilians hurt. In fact, they can't even know what you're doing. Unlike the Ghostbusters, you have to be discreet when you're clearing a hotel."

I didn't mention that I was holding in reserve a request for him to use whatever power it was he'd exerted that had blasted that pack of death eels off his back. I glanced at the bandage on his neck then looked away.

I looked at Andi, who smiled at me shyly but tried to look defiant. "What about me?"

"You? You're hopeless. I'm not even sure why you're on this team."

She put on mock outrage and slapped my shoulder. "That's not true. I contribute."

"Maybe you can find a pattern in their argyle socks or something. Maybe all ghasts wear stripes with plaids, and you'll see it just in time to save us!"

She folded her arms and turned away.

"No," I said gently, "you're there for intelligence and common sense and a level head. Not to mention the ability to bash things with driftwood. You'll be fine, Sweet…heart."

Tank affected a yawn. "So when are we going to do this? First thing after breakfast?"

"No, Colossus, now."

SIMPLY GHASTLY

The thing about ghasts was that they were unpredictable. I hadn't known if Jose the Waiter was going to attack us in my suite or what. And since they often acted without forethought, it meant I couldn't read their intentions.

I sat on my couch, cross-legged, with my phone face up on a pillow in my lap. But my spirit was in a foggy sphere just outside the executive boardroom on the first floor of the DFW Grand Hyatt.

My four intrepid adventurers stood huddled at the door, one behind the other in the order I'd outlined, as if about to storm a dragon's den. Daniel had his fiery spirit sword and Brenda was spewing righteous anger. We even had a tank going first. And Sweet Cheeks was there to beautify and add romantic tension and otherwise round out my little Dungeons & Dragons questing party.

And me…I was dungeon master. What else?

I bent a thought toward the hotel security staff and saw that they were indeed alerted that we were going to be doing some…interesting…things. They were under strict orders not to interfere unless something caught fire or there was blood. Basically, they were crowd control, but I hoped they wouldn't be needed even for that.

"Yes," I said aloud into the phone, "there is one ghast in there. He's posing as hotel staff. Male. A front desk-looking guy with a blue suit and peach tie. But he's not alone, so your first job is to get him away from the others so you can take him down." I moved my view so I was seeing half on their side of the door and half on the other. "Okay, go."

Tank put his hand on the knob lever.

"Hang on," Brenda said.

All our phones were linked in a conference call, and we had cleaned the gift shop out of ear buds, so at least we could communicate without everything being heard by others. It would do until the pro comms arrived.

"What?" I said, trying not to let irritation take me out of my trance.

"How *exactly* is we supposed to 'take him down'? I ain't got no butterfly net, and unless Cowboy's got a nu-cul-ar thingamajig on his back, we got bubkes."

"We went over this, Belinda. You spray your holier-than-thou anger at it, Moose holds it down, Fred Jr. slices and dices it with his sparkle sword, and

Andi stands there looking pretty."

"Ugh," Sweet Cheeks said. "How can you be this *annoying?*"

"It's a gift. But you're right, darlin'. Next time, you stay here and sit in my lap, plying me with grapes and margaritas. No sense risking you."

"Ugh!"

I smiled to myself. "Okay, they're done in there. Moose, step back now!"

He pulled his hand back just as the door swung open, and three of the five staffers walked out. The front-ghast-clerk was still inside, along with a petite Asian dustmaid I might just have to pay some attention to in the near future.

"Okay, go now."

Tank opened the door and they went in, crouched and ready to strike.

"Guys," I said, "this isn't a cage fight. Fly casual."

A huge brown wood table dominated the room. It was basically a table-room. Six black, wide executive chairs sat smartly on one side of the table, facing across the shiny surface to six chairs on the other side. Each place setting had a signing pad like a placemat, a short pad of white paper, a pen, and an upside-down water glass.

Both staffers were on the far end of the room next to a widescreen monitor on the wall. They turned to my adventurers.

The ghast-clerk clasped his hands in a fig leaf pose and smiled. "Can I help you folks?" He even had a Texas accent. Nice touch.

"Tell the dustmaid that someone was calling for her," I said.

Brenda said it, and I listened to the maid's

thoughts. But of course they were in Mandarin. So I took a chance.

"Tell her her boss wants to see her right away. Make it sound urgent."

Brenda did, and the maid said, "Shyeh-shyeh" and scurried from the boardroom.

I wondered if the ghost could see Daniel's flaming sword or if its vision was limited to the natural. I thought perhaps he would play the desk clerk a little longer, but I was wrong.

With a warping shimmer in the remote viewing plane, the young man vanished and in his place was a skinny old woman ghost with a Roaring Twenties haircut and bangles that slid down a radius and ulna barely covered by skin. I didn't know if they'd be able to see the change or—

Smartmouth swore like a Belinda rat, and I had my answer. It was the one she'd drawn, after all.

"Stay back!" Andi sounded more than a little afraid.

They stayed more or less in their line, all hiding behind their tank. For his part, the troll crouched and held his hands apart like lion claws. He advanced on the ghost as if to grapple with it. I couldn't fault his courage, that was for sure. All he had to do was grab it so Daniel could—

The she-ghost doubled in size and flew at Tank with a flurry of slender limbs, claws, and teeth. All he could do was lean back to keep her head in view, and it was on him, shredding his arms and bloodying his nose and already pawing over him to get at someone else.

Tank's blood sprayed over the table and notepads, and the thing screamed like a goat demon. All four of them fell on their rumps in shock and fear. Daniel's sword went out. "Get away! Get away!" someone shouted.

I didn't know they could get big like that. That hadn't happened in Chile. What exactly were we dealing w—

The ghast sprang over Tank, grabbed Daniel above the right knee, and fled the room, bursting the door to shards and carrying the kid upside-down and flailing.

German profanity.

PEAR-SHAPED

So much for discretion.

Brenda ran through the conference wing of the Grand Hyatt screaming Daniel's name. Andi came next, shaking and mumbling, "Omigosh, omigosh, omigosh."

Tank thundered after and quickly passed them both. His wounds seemed to have enraged him, and blood flowed over his arms and mouth and chin. He tore across the carpet, leaving about as much damage than the fleeing ghast. Hotel staff shrank against the walls or fell to the floor when the monster and its pursuers passed.

The ghast had to run crouched to keep its head under the ceiling tiles. I'd never seen one grow like that. This could be a problem. Daniel wasn't shrieking or crying, but he wasn't exactly calm and his sword had snuffed out. The creature ran past tasteful abstract paintings on the wall and stylish banded carpet, slavering and screaming like a sheep hit by a truck. My team came close behind.

I roved ahead to keep up, trying to send a powerful-enough suggestion to security to get involved now. I wasn't sure it would work, and I saw Andi stumble, so I had an idea. "Andi, go to security and tell them there's been an incident and that it's ongoing. Tank needs medical help and we need them to keep people away from the conference wing. Can you do that for me?"

"Of course I can," she said into her phone, getting up and running toward the main lobby. "I'm not a child."

"Wait, are you mad?"

"Just help Daniel!"

I zoomed down the hall as the ghast came to the end of the long conference wing lobby and burst through two sets of double doors that led into the hotel's 400-seat presentation hall. Gray chairs sat in neat phalanxes in front of massive blue video screens flanked by blue curtains.

The creature waded into the high-ceilinged room, pushing chairs aside as if walking through water up to its knees. It slowed a bit and transferred Daniel to its other hand.

That was enough for Tank to catch up. He launched himself at the beast's middle, knocking it forward onto gray chairs and spraying his blood on the fabric. The creature lost its grip on Daniel, who hit his head on the back of a chair and lay still.

Great. Without Daniel's metaphysical sword, I didn't know how we were going to destroy the creature.

The ghost twisted its torso and reached those over-long arms at Tank, but he held tight to its middle. It hammered him relentlessly, but he held tight. Daniel moaned and stirred.

Brenda arrived and ran directly for Daniel. The ghost rolled in its struggle with Tank, tossing chairs aside. But Brenda got to Daniel and tried to pick him up. She wasn't big and he wasn't small, and the angle was bad—plus, physical combat nearby—so she settled for grabbing him under his arms and dragging him back toward the busted doors. He lolled his head around.

I felt so helpless. This was pure chaos and I had no clue how to make a difference. I hated that feeling. I had half a mind to cry out to the Almighty, like some oafish peasant.

I'm okay. It was a thought from Daniel.

Seriously? Awesome! Can you get the sword going again?

In the misty hologram of my RV vision, I saw Daniel's spirit sword flare to life.

The ghost must've seen it too, because it—she?—flailed at Tank to get away. But Cowboy held on, his arms raked by cuts and his face covered in bright blood.

"Daniel, no!" Brenda reached for the kid, but he darted away toward the scrum on the carpet.

The Roaring Twenties slender-hag became frenzied at the approach of the sword. Daniel went into the aisle between the disrupted set of chairs and the pristine phalanx next to them and neared the ghast's head.

Just hack at anything, I thought at him. *It should slice through all parts of her. It's like a light saber.*

He raised the sword over his head and lunged forward. The ghast put up an arm, and he cut it clean off.

The creature shrieked so loud I saw Brenda collapse to the floor with her hands over her ears.

At that moment, on the other side of the huge room, the Hispanic waiter came crashing through the double doors.

With a roar and a ripple of reality, he discarded the illusion of humanity and grew into Slenderman— spindly limbs, an immaculate black tuxedo, and only the barest hint of features on an otherwise blank orb of a face. It was a nightmare creature, and I knew that ghasts in this form had been indirectly responsible for several teenage suicides.

This one seemed more interested in homicide. In its larger size, it consumed the distance to Daniel with astonishing speed.

Now, kid! I thought. *Kill that one now!*

It crossed my mind that I shouldn't be asking a little kid to be a monster-slayer, but at the moment, he was what we had.

Daniel drew back his flaming blade and jabbed it forward into the she-ghast's neck. It struggled and moaned, but Daniel kept at it. He hacked and stabbed and thrust. His hits landed true, but the thing was big and strong, and it was taking too long to die. Slenderman was almost on them.

"Stay back, you devil freak!" Brenda stepped into

the space between Daniel and the other ghast. She had her right hand forward like a superhero crossing guard, and I could feel her shooting a beam of protective, Mama Bear, stay away from my baby anger at the creature.

It flinched and pulled up short, as if struck by a stun gun.

Brenda advanced on it. "Get back, and go back to whatever hellhole you crawled out of. Leave this hotel and never come near any of us again!"

The thing backpedaled and shuddered, twitching as if being tased. But now and again it snarled and surged forward, only to be halted again, and I didn't know how long her trick would work.

I heard a commotion out of the range of my vision, and it wasn't only the sound of Daniel finally lopping the head off of the Charleston Ghast, either.

"I did it!" he shouted.

That broke Brenda's concentration, and she turned to look.

Whatever had restrained Slenderman snapped, and it rushed at her, its blank features stretched and its hands spread into claws.

"Brenda," I shouted at her, knowing I was too late, "watch o—"

Thunder boomed in the cavernous hall, and the ghast was thrown off its path. Its left arm popped Brenda on the side of the head as it cartwheeled over. She fell and it fell, and a squad of security guards advanced, pistols raised.

A fifth figure—Sweet Cheeks!—ran to Brenda and pulled her aside, while the guards closed on Slenderman. It got to its knees but the thunder clapped again, and it fell back under a barrage of bullets.

There was a break in the tension. Medical personnel came to Tank and Brenda and Andi hugged. I could tell they all thought the danger had passed, but I knew differently. *Daniel,* I thought, *cut that one's head off too, just to be sure.*

Okay.

Then even I started to relax. That was when I heard the sound of commotion again, and I realized it wasn't coming from the bilocating vision. It was much closer. I climbed out of the RV trance and opened my eyes.

The third ghast stood over me. Right there in my suite. It was an oversize version of a teenaged Mowgli, shirtless and horribly thin, with long bedraggled hair over its face and those white, white eyes.

"Uh, guys," I said into the phone still on my lap. "I think I'm going to need some help."

TOGETHER AT LAST

I flipped over the back of the couch, sending my phone and the pillow flying, and held my hands out toward the ghast.

"Nice jungle boy. Nice Mowgli."

The ghast looked sullen and slightly slouched, as any gangly teen boy should. But with the eyes all white, I couldn't tell if it was looking at me or not. It breathed heavily, as if it had taken the stairs, but it didn't fly into a rage just yet. It merely towered over me, breathing.

I risked a glance down the short passageway to the door. It was closed and not smashed, so I figured

"Boy" had been posing as hotel staff and had just let himself in before going native on me.

Could I bolt to the door and run?

I looked back at Mowgli, and he hadn't moved. The constrained violence was disquieting, like the Alpha Male mutant in *I Am Legend*. I took two steps toward the door, and the ghast sprang forward to cut me off. It stood in the passageway and pawed at me listlessly.

I backed away. "Okay, okay. I like it here anyway."

What was the thing doing? Was it depressed that its friends had been decapitated? Was it in need of a battery charge?

Was it waiting?

Outside of my remote viewing trance and without my phone, I had no connection to the others. It was possible the phone was still on, though, wherever it had flown to, so I combined a strong mental warning with a spoken one. "Guys, if you can hear me, watch out. I think this thing is waiting for you to get here."

I backed to the desk and scanned it for something I could use as a weapon. Narrow computer speakers? No. Netbook? No. Not even a letter opener. The dining table had been cleaned, but there were knives in the sink. Better than nothing.

I hadn't more than decided it than the thing leapt at me. It crossed the room in a lunge and reached for my neck. I blocked the sickeningly narrow limbs and tried to run behind the dining table.

It slammed a forearm into my right shoulder and knocked me hard against the window overlooking a ten-story drop to the airport tarmac. The glass held, but the blow had knocked me hard. I stumbled toward the table, but the thing made a wet flaying noise and shoved me in the back.

I fell forward behind the nearest dining chair and rumpled the throw rug. The creature bent over me like a human praying mantis, batting me with those hideously long arms.

I scooted away and grabbed a chair leg. I tried to use the chair as a weapon, but the ghast knocked it and the whole table away savagely and fluttered its lips at me, gagging me with stink breath.

It slashed my forehead with with a horizontal swipe of its hand, and I felt cuts open from ear to ear. Blood spilled over my eyebrows and into my eyes.

"Help!" I called, feeling wretched and ashamed of my weakness. How had I—*I*—been reduced to this? And since I was that low, I might as well go lower. "Please," I begged, "please. What do you want? I'll do anything." This was how I was going to end, useless and begging.

The ghast grabbed me by the waistband of my pants and dragged me into the open space in front of the desk. I struggled and kicked its torso and rolled against its grip, but all that did was shake sweat from its dangling locks and make it narrow those white eyes.

It sank its claws into my upper arms and lifted me off my feet. I had a mental image of it simply biting my head off and spitting it out to go bouncing on the pretty parquet floor.

As it brought my face up to its mouth level, time seemed to slow. I saw a memory of Stephie receiving the creatures from my soul and thrashing with their evil. I saw her run away toward the highway. I saw what was left of her on the road.

I saw the things Brenda had somehow gotten

access to from my past, all the humiliations and rejection. The slit of light under the closet door that was my only illumination for what seemed like my entire childhood.

I couldn't even remember the first time he'd hit me. Probably because it had started so early. But I could remember the time he'd done so when I'd brought him a hand-drawn Father's Day card but had apparently chosen an important moment in the TV show to show it to him.

And suddenly this ghost wasn't a jungle boy anymore. It wasn't even a monster from the Gate anymore. It was William Jackson Thorton. My father, the devourer god.

Please…help…me.

The thought shocked me, even in that moment on the doorstep to death. It wasn't a psychic command or even a plea to someone nearby to come to my rescue. It was…

It was a prayer.

The ghost seemed confused. It cocked its head at me and furrowed its brow. Then it seemed to shake it off, and it squeezed its claws into my flesh, ripping the skin and piercing to the bone.

I shouted in pain and surrender to the end.

That was when Mystery, Inc. burst in.

The ghost turned in surprise and tried to drop me, but its claws were stuck in the bloodied muscles of my arms. I came off one of its hands and dangled diagonally from the other, fighting to pull its claws out of me.

A wave of some sort of power washed over me. What I *felt* was Brenda's spiritual anger, but what I *saw* was a tank of a man wrapped in hastily applied bandages and with dried blood on his face running forward like a subway train. He swung a metal table leg at the ghast and connected with the head. I went down with it.

"First the arm!" Sweet Cheeks yelled. "The arm, Tank."

Tank body-slammed the creature's head on the ground and wrested its free arm behind its back. It shrieked and sputtered, and I was able to use my legs now to pull loose from its other hand. It tore a chunk from my triceps, but I was free.

"Now move!" Andi commanded.

Tank scooted down the creature's body and leaned away from its head. Brenda sidestepped to have a clear view. She reluctantly urged Daniel forward.

Daniel held before him an invisible weapon I knew only too well, though it was strange to not be able to see it.

"In the name of Jesus," Tank said—needlessly, I would've argued, except for my own recent petition of the universe—"be gone!" He nodded to the kid.

Daniel brought the unseen blade down in a mighty chop, and somehow that nevertheless cut into the creature's flesh. Its head came partially off its neck, and Daniel put his foot on its shoulder and chopped again, severing the head entirely.

Just like that, it was over.

The beast's body went utterly still. Cowboy stood and touched his forearms gingerly, and I could see blood seeping through the bandages. His neck wound, too, was bleeding a bit. Daniel opened his hands and I knew he'd extinguished the sword. Brenda brought him into a big hug and pulled him protectively from the thing on the carpet.

Andi knelt in front of me. "You're hurt. Forehead and both arms." She looked me over. "Anywhere else?"

I just stared at them all. I couldn't understand what I was seeing.

The troll crouched beside Andi and snapped his fingers in front of my face. He kept doing it until I flinched and turned away. He reached his hands to the wounds on my arms.

"You guys came," I said, hating how dazed and stupid I sounded. I blinked blood out of my right eye.

Andi wiped it away with her finger and then with a napkin Daniel brought her. "Of course we came, Chad. We're a team, aren't we?"

Normally I would have had some smart riposte, but my brain felt like Jell-O. "I knew you guys were, you're a team, but…" I shrugged.

Tank put his hand on my forehead. "That means you too, dummy."

I looked at Smartmouth and asked *you too?* with my expression. She rolled her eyes and smiled.

Daniel gave me a fist bump.

I realized that my forehead didn't sting anymore. I brought my hands up and found smooth skin, not the flayed shoe leather I was expecting. My arms stopped hurting too. I looked at Tank. "Did you…?"

"I didn't," he said, then pointed upward. "But someone did."

"Right." I checked my arms and moved them about. "Thank you. All of you. Thanks for coming when I called."

Epilogue

"What a day!" I said.

The others laughed grimly, like veterans of a military campaign. We lounged in the rooftop saline pool atop the DFW Grand Hyatt, sipping adult beverages—except for Daniel, of course—and watching jets take off into the night sky.

I finished my frozen strawberry margarita and set it on Ashley's tray, which she'd just put in front of me to bring me another of the pink delights.

She swept my hair with her fingers and winked, and I wished she was already off duty. "I'm glad you're going to be with us for a long time."

"Me too, Ash."

Ashley went around to the rest of our group, collecting glasses and handing out fresh ones, then she headed for the elevator. There were a couple of other swimmers here, but she paid them no mind.

Tank sat with his legs in the pool, keeping his arm bandages dry. Apparently, his healing gift didn't work on himself very often. He sat next to Andi, and I cursed the fact that I'd not been able to keep them apart in swimsuits. Still, what was a guy to do? Especially since it had been my idea to have us all live together. It was bound to happen. But curse his sculpted abs!

Brenda hadn't taken her bathrobe off. She sat in a chaise she'd pulled close to where the rest of us sat. Daniel was doing handstands underwater and coming up occasionally for a drink of Sierra Mist.

"I guess that's true?" Brenda said.

I looked at her over my shoulder. "What's true?"

"We're going to be here a long time."

I shrugged. "Unless something better presents itself."

"I don't know," Andi said, swishing her legs in the blue-lit water. "Are you going to be able to live in that suite, after what happened? I don't think I could, no matter how many times they scrub the floor, you know?"

"Yeah," Brenda said, "I keep seeing that thing's neck half chopped through." She shuddered.

I shrugged again. "It's not a problem. And we'll be installing a security system and bringing in specially trained guards ASAP. Anyway, I've seen lots worse than that. You have too, if the stories of your other 'adventures' are even half true. Here, at least we're together, which means safer."

Tank smiled mischievously. "Did you like how we came into your room that time? Just like you'd said: me first, then Daniel, then Brenda, then Andi. Brenda's angry eyes, my muscles, Andi's brain, and Daniel's Masters of the Universe sword. Hoo-boy, that was good. And it worked just like you'd said, that was the crazy part."

I chuckled with the rest of them. "Yes, sometimes even I have a good idea."

We fell silent. Planes landed and planes took off. Daniel came up for air and went back under. The other swimmers left.

"So this is us," Andi said.

"What do you mean?" I asked.

"Us. This is our team now, us five. And here."

I didn't answer this time. My spidey-sense told me to shut up for once.

Brenda sat forward in her chaise. "It's kinda like we're rich."

They smiled and nodded.

"Livin' like queens and kings," she said. "Havin' people wait on us. Orderin' up room service all *day*, y'all. A girl could get used to it."

"And," Tank said, lifting a finger in the air, "the Cowboys' stadium is right here!"

We laughed.

Daniel surfaced and slurped the entire refilled glass of Sierra Mist, chased by a belch. "Brenda...I mean, 'Mom.'"

"Whoo," Brenda said. "Still gotta get used to that one. What is it, sugah?"

"What if I don't like the tutor they're getting for me? I like learning from you."

"Then I'll teach you. But some things yo mamma

don't know how to teach. Aw, you'll be okay, baby."

Andi pulled her legs from the water. "Well, I don't know about the rest of you, but I've had about as much fun as I can stand today." She stood and wrapped herself in a giant white towel. "I'm going to go test out that king-sized mattress in my suite. Good night."

The rest of them departed with her, leaving me to wait another half hour for Ashley to get off work and join me for a swim…et cetera. I'd been moved to the other presidential suite for a day so they could clean my real one. I wondered what they would do with the bodies of the ghasts.

I leaned back in the corner of the pool and nestled my head in the nook. The stars above were dimmed by the airport lights and the glow of the surrounding city, but I could still find the Big Dipper.

Well, Big Fella, I guess I should say thanks. I didn't know how I was going to get them here, but that sort of got taken care of. And when that thing was about to finish me off…

Anyway, yeah. Thanks. And…I guess I'll talk to you later.

Don't miss the other books in the Harbingers series which can be purchased separately or in collections:

CYCLE ONE: INVITATION
The Call
The House
The Sentinels
The Girl

CYCLE TWO: MOSAIC
The Revealing
Infestation
Infiltration

The Fog

CYCLE THREE: The Probing
Leviathan
The Mind Pirates
Hybrids
The Village

OTHER BOOKS BY JEFF GERKE

NOVELS

Virtually Eliminated
Terminal Logic
Fatal Defect
Operation Firebrand—Origin
Operation Firebrand—Crusade
Operation Firebrand—Deliverance

FICTION HOW-TO BOOKS

Plot Versus Character
The First 50 Pages
Write Your Novel in a Month
The Irresistible Novel

For more information about Jeff, visit JeffGerke.com

Made in the USA
Charleston, SC
21 September 2016